Will Badrul Mustafa Never Die?

Verse from the Front

Will Badrul Mustafa Never Die?

Verse from the Front

Heru Joni Putra

translated by
George A Fowler

LONTAR

Jakarta, Indonesia

Jl. Danau Laut Tawar No. 53
Jakarta 10210 Indonesia
www.lontar.org

All artwork, including the painting for the cover and the sketches herein,
by Hanafi.
Design and layout by Cyprianus Jaya Napiun

ISBN No. 978-623-7150-15-2

Contents

Will Badrul Mustafa Never Die?
Verse from the Front

The Beard of Haji Agus Salim

Haji Agus Salim stood
At Heaven's gate
His beard earthward drooping

Badrul Mustafa leaped and sprang,
Trying to catch the beard of Haji Agus Salim,
"With no stairway to Heaven,
The beard of Haji Agus Salim will do,"
Said he.

The hand of Badrul Mustafa snatched
The end of the beard of Haji Agus Salim
He yelled for joy,
And invited his bosom pals
To clamber up that beard.
"Raft to the headwaters,
Swim to the side,
Enter Heaven first,
On to Mecca after,"
Said he.

Badrul Mustafa
His bosom pals

And kith and kin too,
Flocked to climb the beard of Haji Agus Salim
They dangled, they swayed,
And swung this way and that,

Always cheering,
From one age to the other.

Where There Is No Forest, a City Will Do

Always people say,
"When there's no rattan, roots will do."
Well, the rattan has long gone
And there aren't any roots either now.
People seem not to believe
And keep saying,

"When there's no rattan, roots will do."

Maybe such people still don't know
That rattan and roots once available,
Now have become divers shapes and forms
And where once were primeval forest lands
Are now cities
But they've never felt disappointed
Because in the places now urbane
They are still doing
What they usually do in woodlands:
Taking what they need
Without needing to ask.
Because, says Badrul Mustafa,
Whatever's found in cities

Belongs to us all.

Ballad of the Gold-Embroidered Rag

So that eyes could see beyond the skies,
As generations of ancestors advised,
Badrul Mustafa wore briefs on his head

But when the briefs he had shoved
Upward his head he tilted, "*Astaga!* Oh no!"
It was still just the sky,
His two eyes saw it

Not wanting too soon a disappointment
He kept his gaze skyward, "Astaga!"
He saw the sky so blue, the birds
flying without a side glance, but what he saw,
Was the usual view, as always.

"What news, Badrul Mustafa?"
Said a winged horse turd,
Flying in a whirl before him.

Badrul Mustafa did not reply right off
Just observed that winged turd
And only then did he say,
"Good horse turd,
Tell me your name
And why you addressed me."

"My name is Badrul Mustafa,"
Replied the horse turd.
"Badrul Mustafa is my name, friend,
Say what your name is," replied Badrul Mustafa,
"Or I will lick you and spit
At the spinning wind, so you will
Disappear in a trice," he threatened.

"You won't be able
To vanish the horse turd, my Lord,
Horse turds are like soldiers,
Always following wherever you go,
Even if you hide
Behind a stalk of *ilalang* grass."
Replied the horse turd,

"Horse turds are like
The warnings of rulers who keep
Calling and calling your name
Even in your best dreams
So easy is it for horse turds
To become the movers and shakers."

Badrul Mustafa unsheathed his sword
And pointed to the horse turd,
"What do you intend by meeting me?"

The horse turd smiled broadly
And asked Badrul Mustafa
To sheathe his sword,
Then said, "Sir Badrul, would you like
To become our leader?"

Badrul Mustafa again drew his sword.

"I'm only the message bearer," the horse turd said,
"Only you are fit to become
The ruler of the horse turds of the cosmos,"
The turd retorted.

"Lead us by the hand and guide us,
All the horse turds of this world
Back to every Sacred Ass, my Lord"
He went on
So softly.

Badrul now could not say a word
He stared at that horse turd

So devoutly,

And languorously,
The sword loosened from his grip,
Then drops of drizzle fell one by one.
And the air felt like bamboo knives

Now Badrul had reason
For the melancholy of a solitary

He let the horse turd
Stay in the palm of his hand,

Relating that previously he too
Had been a pile of horse turds

Who first was promoted to be
The King's mustache-shiner,
And now commanding general,
And because, he said, he hoped for moon and star,
What he really wanted was to be Poet Laureate.

Dancing on a Weathered Footbridge

Returning from some war,
Badrul Mustafa discovers
A coconut tree
Growing inside his house,

"Tell me,
An envoy from which century
Planted you here?"
He asks the coconut tree.

There is no reply

"Or must I become
A wifeless Padri
Whose birth sword
Easily stands on its own,
Then makes you
Feel you're cut down,
Time and again?"

The coconut tree
Stays mute.

"Or must I become
The sole heir of
Datuk Nan Maraso Ebat Surang
And cut down every coconut
That has just sprouted?"

No reply.

Badrul now with his sword
Scores the coconut tree—
Giving it a pair of eyes,
A relief for an empty stare,
And a too-wide grin.

"Now,
Tell me", he says.

The coconut tree just stays
Silent.

Again Badrul's sword scores the tree,
Making several signs
That mean
I don't hear you!"

"All right! All right!"
Said Badrul,
"I'll give you a pair of
Simple ears."

The coconut tree
Still says nothing
Though Badrul Mustafa
Has repeatedly whispered
An old verse
In his own version,
"There was something of the bending Wau,
And I hope you make it the straight-up Alif…"

Again with his sword he scores the tree
"I will torment you the live-long day,"
Threatens Badrul,
"Until you love me."

Just Call This Poem "Meditation"

On the surface of the pond
Cold air and a slow wind
Reveal their forms to Badrul Mustafa.

Badrul Mustafa heeds
That cold air—
A shepherd
Old and decrepit: throughout time
He has taken his sheep and circled the world.
In search of the Promised Meadow.

Badrul Mustafa stares
At that slow wind—
A soldier
So frail: Throughout the centuries
He has pointed his rifle, circled the globe,
And marched people
Toward the Holy Prison.

Badrul just gazes at the pond
But those who were there aren't there now

Alone and swaying,
He's like a sword
Plunged hastily into the ground.

INDECISIVE

Aren't you all tired?"
Badrul Mustafa tries to summon them.

He feels the air grow colder
and the wind keeps moving slowly.
How much, how so much he still wants
To engage with them.

But since the title of this poem is "Meditation"
Badrul Mustafa
Shuts his eyes again

Heh-heh

Ballad of the Tree Stump

The birds just fly by overhead.
In fact, on Badrul Mustafa's head
Is set the covering of a holy man,
"Don't you all feel
There are those in heaven you pass by,
Just casually, without even a 'Peace be to you,'
At all?" shouts Badrul Mustafa.

Badrul Mustafa wanders the whole day,
Tirelessly walking, from dawn to dawn,
Searching for anyone, not limping,
Hurling exhortations to be his disciple,

Two dogs making love cross
Right before Badrul Mustafa, just like that
In fact the dark glasses of a VIP
Are covering his eyes,
"Woi! filthy dogs, why must it be you
That I've got to see through these glasses?"
Snaps Badrul Mustafa as he
Tosses a big stone at those dogs.

Badrul Mustafa wanders the whole day,
Walking, from dawn to dawn, tirelessly,
Searching for anyone, not limping,
Hurling exhortations to be his disciple,

Sha-la-la, he sees a coconut tree so very tall,
Audaciously climbs to its top
And then sings songs of suicide,

He hopes someone will stop him,

But birds just fly by, nothing special,
Hens are busily looking for their brood
Two cats keep scratching other
And a pair of dogs, still going at it,
Stop their lovemaking.

It’s Out, the Torch in Hand

It’s out, the torch in hand
The moonlight can’t of course be trusted
Badrul Mustafa stops walking
His disciples are overcome with fear

“What is deepest part in this earth, sir?”
A eunuch asks Badrul Mustafa.

And he replies, “I really don’t know,
For me, as far as the eye can see,
That is the deepest, and perhaps
Also be the shallowest,”
“Is there a deepest part of the abyss?”
Now a mendicant asks him in despair.

“Truly it’s not like that. This earth is so deep,
You’ll never see its bottom. My eyes or yours
Can only see as far as the abyss. It’s far beyond the abyss.”
Badrul Mustafa says, ever so slowly, “Whatever its name.”

“Oh, whatever to see it with,” the cripple says,
“And how to get there,” the blind one puts in,

Badrul Mustafa says,
“Do you all remember about the waterfall that wants
To take the abyss to the bottom of the earth?”

They all went silent. Trying to remember, perhaps,

"They never come back,
No matter how many rivers try to follow,"
Badrul Mustafa goes on, ending the discussion.

"What is the tallest thing on this earth, sir?"
The slave asks once more.

But everyone has fallen asleep.

Killing the Court Poet

Badrul Mustafa will never tell
Who had ever intended to murder him,

He really hadn't the heart to, in case they were recorded
By historians as the tribe of his haters.

If you're thinking to kill Badrul Mustafa
You'd just need a drop of indigo into the cup *)

Of milk on his desk, for he still supposes
"a drop of indigo into the milk" is merely a figure of speech.

---

*) This evokes the maxim, "*Karena nila setitik, rusak susu sebelanga*" — "Because of a drop of indigo, a vessel of milk is ruined." This is roughly equivalent to "One rotten apple spoils the whole barrel," together with its implications. In the Indonesian, a heavier emphasis is placed on the relative tininess of the lethal drop.

Ballad of the Torn Sandal

"If I die again,"
Said Badrul Mustafa, "I want
To be born again as an *ulama*'s
Piss.

He'd tell his stories to whomever he'd meet,
From the tribe of burnt stumps
To the clan of the coconut shells,
That he would be happier
As the piss of an ulama
Than as a flower blossom
That had been give divers names
In the hands of a lover.

He'd tell his stories to whomever he came to,
From the clans of the hiltless swords
To the order of the toppled banyans,
That he is no longer willing or able
To become the cut-off jewels of a eunuch
Which move from here to there by themselves
While a dog
casually passes near him,

And even less does he want,
When born in the land of the pig hunters,
To only become a simple marker
Of bad luck which will arrive—
Dog shit stepped on in the morning

Truly, for too long,
Has Badrul Mustafa wanted
To be the piss of an ulama.

So, on the day of his umpteenth death,
He lets his spirit dance on his body
Like a green fly on cow flop
How impatiently he awaits the day of return—

When he wells up in the upturned hands of the prayers,
And drips from mouth to mouth of the sinners.

Badrul Mustafa's Horse, 1

Badrul Mustafa
The coachman of our country,
His horse, once belonged to a Padri,
But if told to gallop,

That horse would prefer to die.

Every time Badrul applied the crop
People would awaken from their sleep,
And pray the horse

Would be good at speaking

But, that prayer was not intended
For the horse to beg a thousand pardons
Of its owner. Rather, when they arrived
Over there across the way, the horse could straightway tell
The lass that Badrul Mustafa

Really loved her.

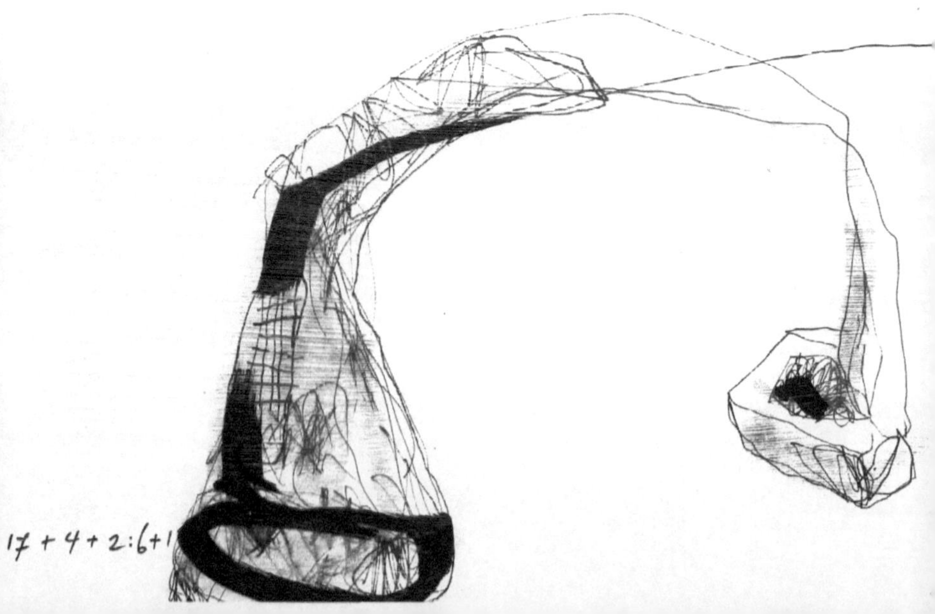
17 + 4 + 2:6+1

Badrul Mustafa's Horse, 2

Badrul's horse broke its promise.

Treading the bridge on the way to a rendezvous
Of the Man and the Maid,

It really didn't want to go any farther.

Being long good with words,
That old horse was only fond of repeating
Stanzas of love once uttered
By a Padri before running from battle,

"The maid tall and lithe
Said to seduce and allure
If never should her ship arrive
On plank of wood I'd pursue for sure."

"On a plank of wood sailing out
Never great waves shall I fear
My heart I keep pumped and stout
From the words of men alone do veer."

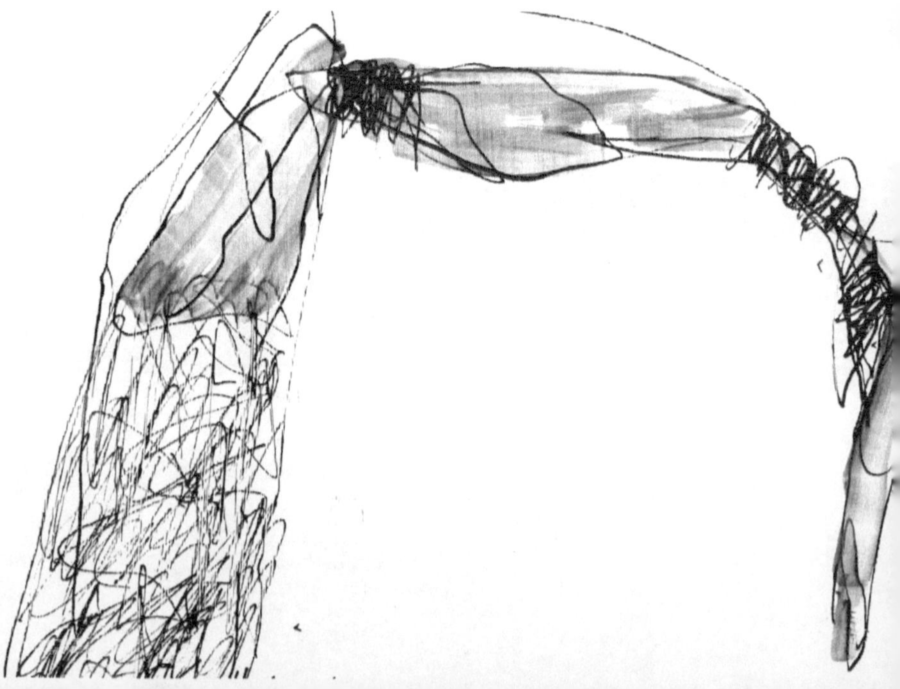

Badrul Mustafa Falls in Love Again

People already now believe
After Siti or Puti
No one else would
Be so loved by Badrul Mustafa.

But God changed his fate—
And now Badrul Mustafa
Loves a banana plant:

Badrul loves a banana heart
Which is rotten inside.
Badrul loves a banana
Ripe, from being fermented

Badrul loves a young banana plant
Cut down before budding.
Badrul loves the petals of a banana plant
Which keep on shedding.

Only the Scent Remains

Badrul Mustafa promises,
With mere applause after the revolt
He would march out of this uncouth land.

It's not at the crossroads that he worries.

"I only wish for no more happiness than I need
My life yet awaits the final episode
Like curry left over when its brazed meat's gone..."

Badrul Mustafa promises
After the love sonnets end for naught
He's out of this fucking country.

It's not the yellow-red spirits of sunset he fears,

"And my love is but a kick,
The final kick of a carriage nag
Before dying standing still on an uphill grade..."

Learning to Recite to a Cow Pen

Since becoming good at inner rebellion,
We were sent to Engku Haji's *surau*.
"In the love tales he would tell,
Stretched forth the road to Heaven." As
Our parents never tired of saying.

But, every time recitations were finished, Engku Haji
Never showed the road to Heaven,
He just always told of the congregation of cows
Who could memorize all the holy books.

We were always told to recite, to search without stopping,

But what we found was only the tiger
Hiding within Engku Haji

We kept on reciting, digging never stopping
But what we found was always the tiger
Which stalked the cows from within Engku Haji,
We kept on reciting, following along ceaselessly
But what we found was still the tiger
Who always roared to keep us away.

Now, every time our parents tell us to recite,
We'd rather to run away. "Let Engku now
Despair at seeing us become
Badrul Mustafa." Better a knife
Stuck into us than a chapel with cows.
"Look, with us Engku only wore sandals
But with the cows Engku wore shoes."
He showed the road to Heaven to the cows
While he just kept us on reciting.

Ballad of the Lunatic Who Mounted the Pulpit

Ever since the lunatic mounted our pulpit
We've been pleased and we've been happy.
Before the women moaned
Verses about paddy planted but *ilalang* grass sprouting
Our crazed fellow began to tell
Of Padang restaurants now built on the moon.
We grew pleased, we grew happy.
He always had a story.
There was also the story about a rich man
Who ate his own filth.
We've been pleased and we've been happy
Ever since our insane fellow climbed the pulpit,
We still leave for the fields
And the kids go to school
Making up *pantun* like mad,
"Far between is Pandan Isle's sound,
Two Goose Isle and more,
Badrul Mustafa lies rotting underground,
A fate for us in store.
Goose Isle out at sea
Behind Two Pandan's land,
What change of fate to see
We plant, but our profit they command."
We're pleased and we're happy.

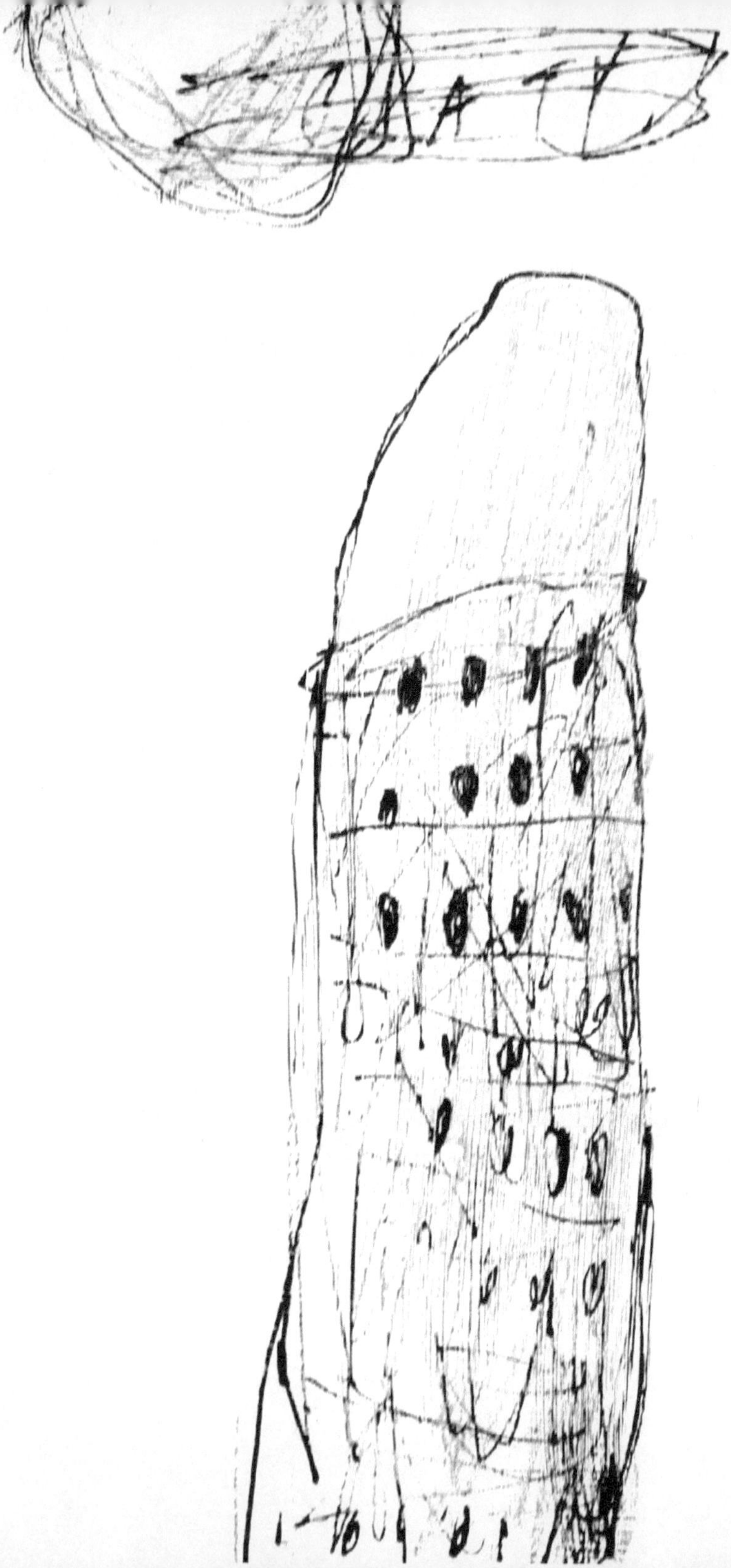

Riding a Shipwreck

Badrul Mustafa enters every market,
Just one guy, swaggering and shoving,
From Monday to Sunday.

His ears prick up to the help-songs of the sellers,
Back and forth the monger of fruit
And the peddler of underwear,
"Buy here, hey kith and kin,
Buy bananas, papayas or watermelon,
But buy their wrappings, hey kith and kin,
At my friend next door..."

And he listens to the rebab boy crooning away
About looming fate,
"Hey, rain, hey, if wet you must be, just drench away,
And don't let the fruit separate from its stalk,
Hey, calamity, if come you must, just do your worst,
Just don't put an end to us five pals..."

Badrul Mustafa enters every market,
Loafing and shambling all by himself,
From morn til dusk.

He's not after alligator-skin shoes,
Morris hats, or shirts
Unbuttoned at the top,
Like what bookies wear at horse races,

Nor looking for ruby-red lipstick,
Talismans from coconut shells,
Or the chicken-shitty smell of shrub verbena
Applied by certain polyandrous singers.

Badrul Mustafa by himself
Is only looking for a strand of thread.
But even if he gets a strand of thread,
Which people say can be used
To bind a wandering memory to the body,
Or to bring home
The sweetheart too long out walking,

A Badrul Mustafa
Will only use that one strand
As a musical instrument to accompany Big Mama
Dancing the joget OMG! the night away.

Ballad of the Man Who Was an Admirer of Jibril

All the pamphlets about
The Coming of the Savior
Have turned out to be pure fiction

He's not coming back

Even in stanzas
Of something Which Will Not Be Seen,
He was never given a narrative.

Then people
Vowing within themselves,
To erase the genealogy and lineage
That have been twined and woven for him,
And let the historians question
All the records about him,

And with determination,

Paint each poetic stanza blue
Which—people say—was written by him

So as not to be reread
In the skies on any morning.

But a man came
Announcing himself,
"My name is Badrul Mustafa.
I am a man, an admirer of Jibril;
My words, at least, will be partly true."

People crowded around him
As they would a commanding general
Standing there dead on the battlefield
"It might be that I'm that savior,"
Badrul pronounced.

Sad to say,
Badrul Mustafa did not ride a horse,
So that no one would imagine
He came as a knight surviving
A war lasting years.
And Badrul also did not journey far like a traveller would have,
So that anyone would belong to
Those exaggerators
When singling out help to him above all else

Then, to him, people again told stories
About the Savior who had been reported
As coming to that country,

"In fact, he was a man who was stoned to death
In the Cave of Nothing and he was a drifter
From the Valley of Perhaps."

Badrul listened; and in nodding,
He shook his head.

Really, he is only
The main character from a tale,
Who with God's permission,
Would never be created."

Badrul listened; and in lamenting
He laughed.

The Song of the Sword Grinder

It's not like me to be afraid of you,

You order me to whet your sword
But I won't blunt the blade of your foe,
You ask me to lengthen your sword
But I won't soften the sword of your foe,
You force me to quicken your sword
But I won't retard the sword of your foe,

I'm not the sort to obey you

The glint of your blade on my neck
Now will never be what you want,
But later what I do will be caused—
Caused by the flame in my eye,
Fearing you is unlike me,
The crackling of my bones
Now will never be your greatness,
But what I do will be the norm

Entirely the norm for the Badrul Mustafas of my era.

Song of a Farmer without a Field

You, holy as you are, may beseech God
That you might own those fields wet and dry
Please go ahead, prophesy
That you'll knock down this old hut,

These fields wet and dry are not my inheritance
I'm really just a paddy planter
That old hut isn't mine
I only need it for lying down on occasion

You, strong as your army is, can entertain
A desire to own those fields wet and dry
You may prophesy
That you're going to knock down this old hut,

But you won't be able to

Snatch away the hoe

In my lap.

To seize my hoe handle
—the strongest, longest, and hardest—
In my lap
You, no matter how Badrul Mustafa you are, won't be able to.

A Storyteller without Applause

One night, in the dark of the moon,
Jibril flew low, just coasting,
And met a child of man, sitting cross-legged,
At the highest point, a blade of *ilalang*

Seeing Jibril coming
The fellow wept,
"Your servant truly is not happy
When the audience for your servant's stories
Are only Badrul Mustafa's people
Who come in swarms,
And yet know not how to clap their hands..."

Jibril stroked the man's head.

"When you are silent," said Jibril,
The words within you move properly
But when you speak, those words bump into each other,
Rebelling, as if wanting to find another tongue
For themselves."

"But," he said,
"Aren't these the stories that I myself have created?"

"Yes, but only when you are silent," said Jibril,
"The words within you march together in ranks,
But whenever you speak, those words wander off,
And wish you would make me
The sole tongue of each word
You want to convey."

The child of man was silent.

Jibril's prophesy wasn't really strange,
But he understood,
After that day,
The cheers for him would recede.

"All right then, now you be the storyteller,"
In the end he conceded,
With a question
Which lacked conviction,

"But are those followers of Badrul Mustafa
Listeners of truly humble heart?"

Ballad of the Paper Lion

A pulpit, and I'll give you choice stories, unusual ones
Or whatever, just don't call it fake news, about a man
With a holy book in hand, sent to a country filled
With these droning laments — where you all decorate yourselves,
To become a savior for whomever for whatever reason
Has forgotten that to enter heaven you must be registered on Allah's Road.
So believe, please believe, and acknowledge that the truth is
That envoy is me, that really there was no one before or will be after me,
Do you all be willing to believe in everything I impart to you,
And not the slightest misleading news do I bring. But before the story begins,
Do you know, like the people before you, to gain the title
Thus, of those on Allah's Road is not easy, unless you answer yes every time I ask:
Will you surrender your belongings after hearing all my tales?

Ballad of the Deer with the Broken Leg

So often do you entreat us, like a peddler of scripture,
To immediately take in your stories, even if we don't know
From whence your steps began. So listen first
To each and every lament we croon, before you persuade us
The envoy is actually you. Or you're just an itinerant preacher,
And having run out of provender, you've headed this way,
Claiming to be the one and only envoy so that
We'll collect money for you. But, remember, you'll never be seen
As a savior here, in a cursed land told of by those tribes bygone
Unless you tell from whence you set out,
So as not to have stretched you legs this way in vain, and so
that you really
Understand how to convey word by word
Your alifs, lams and mims to us here, o savior of our very own.

Ballad of the Monkey Who Got a Toy, 1

Badrul Mustafa recalls the story of the one before him
When first he found a mirror.
His predecessor claimed when looking into it,
He really didn't understand why there was a creature
Who didn't want to talk but always seemed ready
To join in every time he spoke,

But Badrul Mustafa even less understood
Why when first he came across a mirror
His predecessor was merely busy telling
About himself to that creature. It could just have been
The creature also wanted to tell something
To that forerunner of his.

So, the first time he saw the mirror,
Badrul Mustafa held his tongue on purpose
And just stayed face-to-face with that creature.
Like that for hours, until he witnessed
Behind its two eyes stretched
Kilometers of road (and straightway thought
Of how many eateries could be set up at each crossing)
And how,

How not wanting to end fruitless, like his predecessor,
Badrul Mustafa invited the creature
To a coffee shop to talk about something.

Ballad of the Monkey Who Got a Toy, 2

Never could Badrul Mustafa
Tell right hand from left,
So it was impossible for him
To be counted among the war-lovers.

"No big deal..."

Badrul Mustafa was really of course more suited
As a firm adherent—

Ever since his tongue fluently pronounced all-purpose prayers
To wherever he journeyed,
He always raised his two palms heavenward,

"O, dear God,..."

And whenever a dog barked at him,
He would still be the person who'd just pass on by,

Because he'd long known:
What every dog in the world wants,
Apart from making love out in the open,

Is to enter heaven.

Speaking of which,
The tribe of dogs indeed were always asking
Badrul Mustafa,
"We'll keep your feet clean,

But permit us to join
The troupe of your loyal disciples,
Even if it's way in the back."

That tribe of dogs knew
The very front ranks of the loyal disciples of Badrul Mustafa
Were of course only intended
For whoever believed that God
Created the two hands of Badrul Mustafa
Naturally to face upward for prayer always,

Not for holding weapons
And not even for pulling up the underdrawers
That had sagged to his knees.

And also not for throwing a stone
At lying dogs who had previously gone looking for sex
Hither and yon.

At the Tomb of a Padri

Before you I liken myself
To a speck of dust, in accordance with all the poems
Of praise and eulogy your disciples so sweetly intone,
But they say how terribly conceited I am
Even when comparing myself only to a speck of dust
I'd then feel how closely I cling to you.
I once said I was tiny pebble
But that made your spirit seem tiny.
I've announced myself as a chunk of coal
But that made your wisdoms too simple.
Perhaps of course dust is all there is
To adorn me in your presence.
But as your loyal interpreters said,
I hasten too much to achieve the level of dust.
I'd like to compare myself to unbleached cotton
But I wouldn't want to be seen as purer than you.
I want to liken myself merely to an heir of heaven,
But I wouldn't want you to feel
I'm trying to rival your Badrul Mustafas of all time.

On the Day of the Execution

General Badrul Mustafa
Raises his hand
Before the first rifle
Is fired at his head,

"Not one of you
Is going to ask me for
My last request?"
Asks he.

Badrul Mustafa waits
And no one wants to ask.

Still, he voices
A last request,
"Please first put out
The passion of love in my breast!"
Says he,

"The corpse in the grave weeps
Not over a ravaged body
But because the passion of love in its breast
Still smolders."

His executioners don't understand,
But they can sense
General Badrul Mustafa's violent trembling.

But the general is trembling
Not from the dozens of rifles
Aimed at his head,
But because there before him stands
People,
Like them,
That is, people
Who'd never understand
That the passion of love
Is the blaze of fire at the bottom of the ocean
And cannot be put out all that easily.

Standing before such people
It's no wonder General Badrul Mustafa shakes:
Were there no threat of rifles by the dozen,
He'd surely try to escape,
And even if he weren't shot
Surely he would fall down dead by himself.

An Elephant Across the Sea and an Ant Across the Sea

An elephant across the sea
And an ant across the sea

Said the elephant
In the eyes of Badrul Mustafa
"I see him, but now he has arrived
across the sea."

Badrul asks the elephant,
"Who have you seen
Across the sea?"

Replies the elephant,
"I see an ant."

Badrul Mustafa asks again,
"What is it doing, the ant
Across the sea?"

Replies the elephant,
"I see it carrying a grain of sugar,
And then taking it across one sea
On to another."

Badrul Mustafa clears his throat.

Badrul Mustafa's guards chase
An ant across the sea
And interrogates it.
"Was what the elephant saw
In the eyes of Badrul Mustafa,
Was it you?"

Replies the ant,
"Indeed, what the elephant saw
Wasn't me, but another elephant."

Badrul Mustafa's disciples
Report this to the elephant.
But the elephant disputes it.
"Not possible he saw another elephant,
Because surely he'd see a long trunk
And broad ears."

The ant says that what the elephant saw
Across the sea was another elephant
And only because it looked so very small,
The elephant just believes
That what he saw was an ant.

The elephant insists that ants will always be seen
Whether in one's eyes
Or across even the farthest sea.

The ant holds firm.
Elephants are elephants and ants are ants,
Whether they are reflected in the eyes
Or even across the seas.
"It's just that," he goes on,
"An ant across the sea
Is more often mentioned by Badrul Mustafa,
Than is an elephant across the sea. Than is..."

Spellbound by a Tiger

When you call my name just once:
You want me to run like a horse,
But I can only walk like a deer
And you say, "Oh, that's all right."
For you, horse, deer, what's the diff?

When I pass in front of you every day:
You want me to crouch like a pig
But I can only rear up like a cow
And you say, "Whatever. Cow or pig,
The important thing, they both make sounds."

Because my ancestor was a serving wench
You want me to attend to you whenever
I say, "I'm your sweetheart, not your maidservant,"
You say, "Those words both end in –t, don't they?"

Because you don't pay attention to me anymore,
I'm sure you've been spellbound by a tiger,
You say quite impossible! "Badrul Mustafa's only
Been taken in by a woman who's younger." I say,
"It's the same," Then you ask, "What proof?"
I want you to first answer, "Hugging
"And pouncing are equally spellbinding, aren't they?"

You choose to laugh. And go sprawling, resisting, helpless.

Frog on a Coconut Shell *)

As his feet kept stepping ahead,
Badrul Mustafa let a frog
Sit on his shell-like skull,

"What's he there for, sir?" his disciples asked.
"Maybe there's something it would like to hear," Badrul replied.
"Not just about the weather, but also about a saying
That has long mentioned him."

While the cane in his hand
Turned aside the robe of each servant and slave
Whom he met, Badrul Mustafa allowed
A frog to sit on his skull,
"What does he want, sir" asked his disciples.

"Maybe he sees the rain has stopped," Badrul replied,
"So that he doesn't need to take shelter inside the coconut shell..."

"...It's a saying," he went on.

---

*) A play on the simile, "*Seperti katak di bawah tempurung*,"—"Like a frog under a coconut half-shell"—a way of describing someone of limited experience and crabbed, narrow-minded thinking.

A Body That Doesn't Know Itself

Riding on a sliver of bamboo
It's not a grip he wishes for,
Carried away on a strong current
It's not a riverbank he asks for
Dragged down by a whirlpool
It's not something to grab he longs for

Badrul Mustafa only wishes
To be understood as a soul.

Not as a body
"Created for who knows what..."

To be given a serving at a table
Only to be viewed by him
A soul can enjoy by itself
All the laid-out crispy and spicy snacks.

"This body is such a disaster,
Skin and bones, of course, on purpose I
Let my eyes not see anyone
Let my hand not beckon to anything
Because the body is completely useless."

Climbing a mossy tree
He's never been afraid in the slightest
Reaching the top, his knees don't shiver
Rather he summons the storm

Falling from the tree
Is his obligatory worship
Three bones broken
Is the pillar of his faith,
Moaning and groaning
Are his prayers of praise.

"The moment this body is destroyed,
Let my soul be set free,
This body is merely there,
How then to find bliss."

"For the soul that can never die
A gulp of toddy would never be enough at all
For the body which knows not itself
A night journey awaits."

Just Like Badrul Mustafa

My God flips my heart upside down and back again

It's easy for me to hit my head on door jambs—
All praise for the torch in hand
It's easy for me to stumble against wood stumps—
All praise for the moon at night,

My God flips my heart upside down and back again

Deeply I wish to return my turmoil to the waves
Truly I want to surrender my trembling to the fierce winds

My God flips my heart upside down and back again

Standing strong like a banyan in the market square
To be brought low by a passing breeze.

A Thorn in the Flesh

"I scatter every seed into my flesh
Hoping they'll grow to be pure jungle.
So friends will always be within it,"
If it becomes thickets and brushwood? No problem
And if prairies of ilalang? What to do?
But its seeds are actually known as thorns
And thorns are supposed to be destroyed by fire,
"But fire,"
What's more, burns the forest primeval
Poems of passion,
And in fact fire burns thickets and brushwood
Parables of love
And it then burns the ilalang lands
Young offerings,
"And leaves only
Badrul Mustafa within it..."

At a Café

A green bottlefly
Perches on the rim of Badrul Mustafa's cup,

Before leaving the coffee shop
Whistling, whistling,
He breaks off the stem of a flower
And asks the shop owner to place it
Carefully on the rim of his cup of coffee
Bearing the picture of that leader of the revolution.

A Badrul Mustafa
Could never disturb
A fly on pilgrimage.

The Rubaiyat of a Wanderer's *Kopiah*

"These spices are not in the treatise, but they're not just any spices,"

We really did know
You, Sir, would sail here by prahau
But permit us to ask:
How would so big a prahau be built?

But you, Sir, really need to know
Engku Badrul Mustafa needs not a prahau
So, may it please you, Sir, if we also enquire
How can our Engku arrive in Mecca first before all the others,

"This kopiah is not recorded by historians, but it's not just any kopiah."

With nothing but a kopiah
Does Engku Badrul arrive in Mecca
But how then would he cross the ocean
If You desire this kopiah as a gift?

"If you want what you've found please do buy it, sir,"

Our verses won't record an arrival of looters
If, you Sir, are only seeking spices
But if you carry off that kopiah as well
We will display your name, Sir, in each stanza with a curse and a hex

"Therefore, if you wish to go home bearing blessings, turn back now."

Unto the seas with their crazed waves a kopiah was surrendered
With but one utterance, that of *Bismillah*,
Not a buffeting, rather a swaying, not a capsizing, rather a floundering,
"May the great prahau not be overturned, oh searchers of spice,"

Not a floundering, rather a capsizing, not a swaying rather a buffeting,
God's mandate is given with that *Bismillah*, so quibble not nor cavil,
The seas will look not for trouble, nor will storms violate this command
"Then the waves, so matter how crazed, will merely give fright,"

"So long as these do not kill do not take them to heart,"
Because when unfurled, *Bismillah is Infinite*
The sea with its crazed billows will know and resolve
Not to be affronted because a kopiah conducts an Engku on the hajj.

"And when spices are needed, please do come,"
Those in the depths of the sea made crazy by the waves, believe thou this,
They won't be fortunate again, truly never again,
If not knotted by *Bismillah* and not taken aback by curses.

Return of the Adept

Badrul Mustafa now stands
On the road back of an Adept

Not a sprout can grasp him
Not a stem can hold him back.

"But on his head is always the velvet fez,"
Say some. What's dearer to him than life itself perhaps
Is still bound up on dry stumps.

"But sartorial pursuits are his body's delight,"
Some say. Perhaps in the ashes of a stove,
His spirit shall be quite content to reside.

Now Badrul Mustafa stands
On the road back of an Adept.

Today his ass is in your face.
In the heavens he's sure he's got a place to hang.
On the earth he's certain of a toehold.
"The falling tree won't wait
To slam you back on the ground," someone whispers.
"The rotten bridge never tells
Of letting you drown in the sea," whispers someone.

Salt and Ants *)

Where there's sugar that's where the ants are,
Someone said to Badrul Mustafa.

The sugar's all gone, said Badrul, and the ants
Dumped into the sea: this shallow poetry.

*) A play on the maxim "*Ada gula ada semut*"—"Where there's sugar, there are ants."

Prawn Before a Stone *)

Not sure what stone
It was, hidden by the prawn
Behind its carapace.
Badrul Mustafa supposed it
To be perhaps just an ordinary one
That people would talk about,
A stone you'd only find in those old rhymes.
But if just one of the ordinary ones,
Thought Badrul Mustafa,
It's unlikely our prawn would want
To loiter around in front of it for so long.
He was sure there was something
About that stone.
Or maybe, he thought, it was a suspicion stone,
Placed there like an ordinary one.

---

*) A play on the maxim "*Ada udang di balik batu*" – "There's a Prawn Behind the Stone." This means that there is more than meets the eye. Here the poet changed this to "*Ada udang di balik batu*" – "There's a Prawn Before the Stone" – perhaps to imply that there is less than meets the eye.

Waiting for the Fighters to Enter the Arena

While waiting for the fighters to arrive,
Badrul Mustafa went to the center of the arena,
Drumming and singing,

"This is no story about a love unrealized,
But a tale of the efficacies of a clever monkey,
Who could climb any tree
And who was unafraid of to taking on any creature's challenge."

The voices of the fighters were still out of hearing,
Badrul Mustafa kept on with his crooning and storytelling ,
Entertaining the cheering claque now arrived,

"Even though his body was smeared with *gelamai* oil
The monkey will still get to the top of the coconut tree,
Even though pitted against a gibbon tall and slim,
Don't ask to whom misery came first."

The cheerleaders were now in place,
But not a single fighter was to be seen,
Badrul Mustafa didn't worry about running out of stories

"The clever monkey very much disliked being dandified
Always refused to wear dark glasses
And for sure no cowboy hat was ever on his head
And a pistol need not be strapped to his backside."

Badrul Mustafa stopped his chant for a moment
But his hands kept beating the drum,
His pals thought the fighters had arrived,
But Badrul Mustafa went back to singing again.

"The clever monkey disliked posing
He only wanted to be seen as he appeared
But when people swarmed around, he'd start kicking
And if no one came near, he'd still keep his distance."

The day was getting late, the fighters never came
The cheering section went home
Badrul Mustafa was force to finish his song
With a pantun of the chicken in the coop,

"The coops hold many a crowing cock,
The kind who'll fight to their death
Released fly straight to the paddock
Then pinions crippled, all crowing bereft of breath."

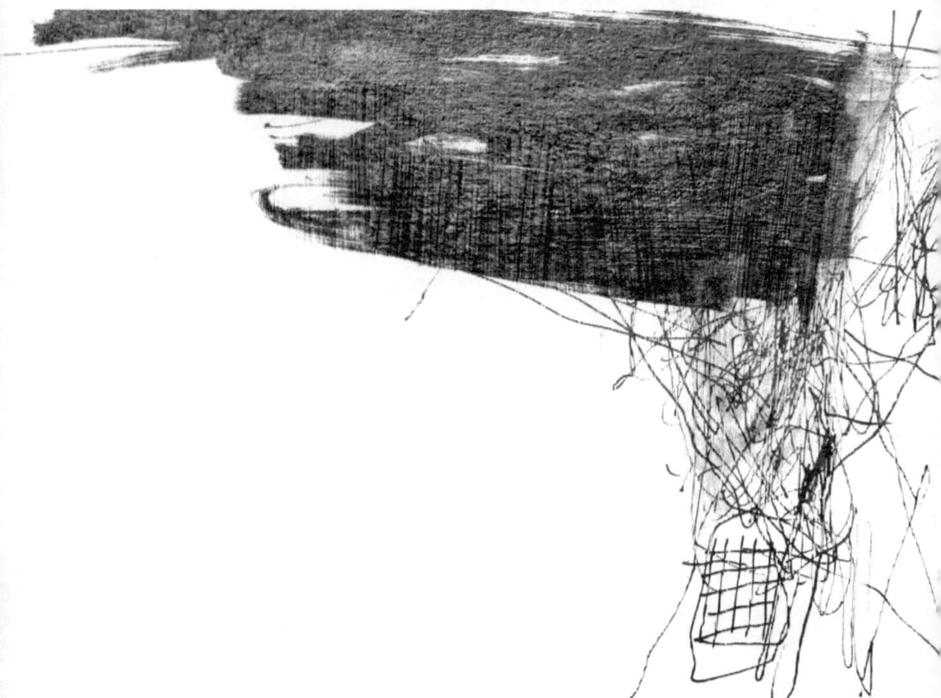

Padri Cheerleader

Since becoming a cheerleader of the Padri,
Badrul Mustafa won't go anywhere

When closing the window
He won't look right or left
Let alone simply greet his own neighbors

Because all movements,
Shambling steps, hunched backs,
Waving hands, beaming eyes.

Feel like someone is always watching.

"The downpour, my dear,
Ends up in the sea,"
Says Badrul, "But why now,
Is everything pouring into this yard…"

Badrul peers from behind the ventilation,
"Pile up the garbage, mud and the dead snake,"
He says, "I'm sure they're trying to surround our house."

Since remarrying,
Badrul Mustafa won't go anywhere,

When opening the window,
He straightway draws the curtain,
And disappears
Into the house.

Because everything is hyper,
Painted smiles, constrained breathing,—
Parted hair, a blinking eye

It feels like someone is always suspecting.

"That coconut tree, my dear,
Has stood straight and tall since back when,"
Badrul says, , "But, why now...."

Badrul peers out from behind the curtain,
"That coconut tree is tilting toward our house,"
He says, "It must want to find out all the secrets
That I tell you..."

Badrul Mustafa Will Never Die

Even though you compare him
To a banana tree
And then yourself
To a Padri on a horse
With a long sword
And then you cut it down again and again,
So, be advised,
He won't ever die,
Because he is Badrul Mustafa.

When your left hand
Only leads a spavined nag
And your right hand
Only grasps a long sword,
Then, you can't just outright
Liken Badrul Mustafa
To a banana tree,

Because just a banana tree
Doesn't suffice to capture
The entirety of a Badrul Mustafa:
Only the passion within him,
Can be likened
To a banana tree—
Once full grown
Killing it is straightway prohibited.

So, whatever there will be about you
And whoever will be like you,
You must bring him low
As a Badrul Mustafa.

Really, it's not wrong for you to search,
You are thinking every day,
And you watch where he goes,
Until you find
What you will give him that's like you.

For example, one day who knows when
You find him
A fierce-looking soldier
Who standing in a long rank,
With measured pace heads into battle,
So you can liken yourself
As just a pebble
In his shoe.

Or on some day or other
You find him
Exhorting the congregation,
So don't hold back, let alone fear being wrong,
If you really want to liken yourself
To the cheese-layered horseshit
Coming out of his mouth.

Felling a Banyan Tree

You'll never be able to topple
The banyan tree in the middle of the market,
Only by averting your face from it
And then saying to everyone you meet
As far as you're concerned, it isn't there.

And you'll never be able to topple
The banyan tree in the middle of the market,
Even though an axe
You swing again and again against its base
And then you stop, just like that
When those who know history say
What you are doing
Is simply impossible because your ancestors
Had tried to bring down
That banyan with a boulder
But it's still stood strong
Right to your time
So you won't ever be able to overturn
The banyan in the middle of the market unless
You bring all your uncles and cousins, pals
And bosom-buddies, and swing all the axes
At the base of that banyan, as you caper
And sing, and never stop swinging, axe
Upon axe against its base, and with them
Imagine when the banyan topples over,
All wide eyes watching, with them
You create…Whoa, wait a sec,

Together? Doesn't that word still sound strange
In your two ears? As Badrul Mustafa, is there
Anything more valuable to you in this world
Than being alone?

Glossary

Bismillah
(Arabic) "In the name of Allah,"

Engku
A term of respect in Minangkabau country for one's maternal uncle or grandfather, or someone of a higher social status relative to the speaker.

Gelamai
An oily sweet made of pounded sticky rice, coconut, salt and sugar.

Haji Agus Salim
The West Sumatran Haji Agus Salim (1884–1954) was one of the great figures of the Indonesian nationalism movement and the early post-Independence period. Over his long career he was not only a journalist, diplomat and statesman, and an influential and revered advocate for modernization of Indonesian Islamic society.

Ilalang
A kind of cogon grass (*Imperata cylindrica Raeusch*), a coarse vegetation which often forms savannahs after destruction of rainforest cover.

Jibril
Christians know Jibril as the Archangel Gabriel.

Kopiah
The shorter Indonesian and Malay version of the traditional fez of the Middle East and Maghrib countries.

Padri

Spelled "*paderi*" in Indonesian and derived from the Portuguese, "*padre*". In seventeenth-century British India, this term primarily referred to Christian ministers and missionaries, but over time was extended to non-Christian clergy as well. In the Indonesian context, "Padri" was the term given to Muslim scholars from Minangkabau West Sumatra who, upon returning from sojourns or pilgrimage in Wahhabi-influenced Arabia, proselytized energetically to expunge customary law (*adat*) from Minangkabau life and replace it with the Sharia canon of Islamic law. This was fiercely resisted by *adat* adherents, and the internal strife from 1803 to 1837 known as the Padri Wars eventually resulted in the *adat* chiefs and royalty inviting the Dutch to side with them against the Padri in 1821, which finally tipped the balance on the side of the *adat* community. In the following decades the Minangkabau world managed to accommodate both adat and sharia in daily life, a modus vivendi that continues to this day. Here the poet is using the term "padri" with contemporary religious hardliners in mind.

Pantun

A traditional epigrammatic quatrain, invariably with a ABAB rhyming pattern.

Surau

A diminutive mosque, a kind of "chapel," found largely in Sumatra and Malaysia. It serves the various congregational functions of a mosque, except that the main Friday prayer is not held there.

Ulama

A Muslim religious scholar. Although this Arabic word is widely understood as a singular-number noun in Indonesia, it is the actually the plural form of "alim" ("the learned one," scholar).

The Poet and the Translator in Conversation

GAF: How did you come to write this collection of poems centering on the enigmatic and undoubtedly flawed person you call Badrul Mustafa?

HJP: The idea of Badrul Mustafa came to me first in 2013. At that time I was trying to reread Indonesian poetry. One of the things I found and also only then realized was that, in the subject matter, Indonesian poems were dominated by "I," whether the "I" of the poet himself or herself ("I" as poet) or "I" as the subject in the poem (the egocentric "I"). There are only a very few Indonesian poems that use "we" (whether inclusive or non-inclusive), or use certain names.

I felt that such dominance was a problem, at least for the age I live in. The problem for me was this: When I started to learn poetry in primary school, it was defined only as "the expression of personal feelings," another kind of form of "diary entries." In my adult years, that seemed to be the definition of poetry wherever I looked. Perhaps due to the impact of defective teaching of literature in Indonesia, over time, "poetry as an expression of personal feelings" became a sort of collective memory. Even later when I majored in literature at the university, many students and even lecturers still used this paradigm. And I would feel exhausted because every time I wrote a poem, people would frequently see the egocentric "I" in my poetry as being "me," the poetic "I." My poetry was being hemmed in by that interpretation and understanding and it was tiring. So I wondered, "If everything is only personal expression, where is the position of thoughts in my poetry? Where is the socio-political perspective? Where is the craftsmanship?" And so forth. Essentially, for me poetry is more than merely "diary entries." All this compelled me to think of how to find a solution. One way would be to abandon the I-tradition and explore a new form. At that time I wanted to create a fictitious character in my poetry. By creating a character, I would not only be dropping the I-tradition but would be gaining a territory of aesthetic exploration that was wider than the earlier tradition.

What kind of a character would I create? Well, that depended on what I wanted to write later. Finally, after thinking about it for a long time, I decided to name that character "Badrul Mustafa".

GAF: Why Badrul Mustafa? Does this name hold any particular significance for you?

HJP: Even when I was young, I was wary of Islamic fundamentalism. In my neighborhood, we'd call Islamic groups who espouse that sort of thing *buya kompor*. *Buya* is a respectful term of address for someone who possesses religious knowledge, while *kompor* is a small stove or cooker. So *buya kompor* is a term for a religious community who only heat things up with their provocations, incitements, libels, and so forth. As a Minangkabau of West Sumatra, where there is a history with the Wahhabi-inspired Padri movement of the 19th century, I feel uneasy and cautious with such groups.

Over the past ten years, the issue of Islamic fundamentalism has reappeared in Indonesia. My alertness and caution about this, long a part of me, also revived. However, this time, my alertness and caution were supported by a deeper knowledge. To put it differently, the reappearance of these new Wahhabi-style groups in Indonesia finally made me think about something: heroism. These groups always position themselves as heroes bringing salvation, which for me is just plain silly. They appear with their many supporters and say they are going to save the world with "their" truth. Indonesian society is now being squeezed between limited traditional values and unfinished modernism. And those arrogant groups come bringing the promise of salvation. I am not comfortable with this at all. As a poet, I thought of presenting an anti-hero: Badrul Mustafa.

I chose the name Badrul Mustafa for ironic effect. Badrul Mustafa is a beautiful name in Arabic, suitable for a leader. The two words derive from Arabic, with "badr," meaning "the full moon" and "Mustafa," something like "the chosen one." Thus I seem to make Badrul Mustafa the personification of the leader, "the chosen one who brings enlightenment and the truth of religion." But, ironically, this name differs greatly from the behavior or character of its bearer, who is really an anti-hero. And thus, an exemplary name does not mean exemplary behavior. In Indonesia, people are too ready to trust in superficialities like names and do not discern things of higher quality. Lots of people with Arabic (that is, Islamic) names are considered good, religious, and so on, simply for that reason. I show this irony by giving the anti-hero the name Badrul Mustafa.

GAF: In the original Indonesian-language publication in 2017, the title was simply Badrul Mustafa's name repeated three times. What was your thinking there?

HJP: I repeated it three times to indicate a clear pluralization. We can discover Badrul Mustafa in each of the 41 poems contained in that book. There are many Badrul Mustafa's with various forms, functions and modes of presence. In other words, Badrul Mustafa is really a plural subject. In Islam, repetition three times is used as the plural marker; and as when we practice *dhikir*, intoning the name of God, we also pronounce it a minimum of three times. I used this logic for the title to this book in its Indonesian version.

I did this to create an ironic effect. Usually, names that are read out three times in succession are names of grandeur in the Islamic tradition, such as the name of the Prophet. However, I used it for the name of Badrul Mustafa, who clearly is an anti-hero, a fool, absurd, and so forth, as my criticism that, in Indonesia, arrogant people—people who think that only they are right, but for the most part are fools, such as the Wahhabi followers—are adulated like the Prophet.

GAF: Why in at least two instances, "Badrul Mustafa's Horse" and "Ballad of the Monkey Who Obtained a Toy," were these titles used twice, for two different poems? Perhaps these two pairs are somehow linked?

HJP: There are six poems that I treat specially and these are divided into three groups: The two poems titled "Ballad of the Paper Lion" and "Ballad of the Deer with the Broken Leg" are written as a dialogue, one with the other. I signify the "Paper Lion" as a ruler who no longer has authority to dominate and "the Deer with the Broken Leg" as the common folk who no longer have power. Thus, these verses act as a kind of antiphon, speaking back and forth. In fact, in the Indonesian versions, the beginning letters, read vertically, reveal B A D R U L M U S T A F A.

The two poems titled "Ballad of the Monkey Who Obtained

a Toy" are my attempt to show how one metaphoric image can be signified quite differently. "The monkey who obtained a toy" is a trope well-known in the Minangkabau lands for someone who forgets who he really is (*lupa diri*) when getting something new, a kind of excessive euphoria over something new without thinking of its impact and implications. I intentionally used this title for different poems to demonstrate the relative meaning of a single metaphor. A metaphor can be used to explain differing conditions. Even conditions that are diametrically the opposite can be conveyed with the same metaphor. In today's context, I often see how a traditional metaphor is used to legitimize fundamentalist Islamic values and at the same time those of moderates or other entirely different values. Or how the same metaphors are used by two opposing camps to attack each other. I tend to see this case as a weakness of traditional metaphors, like "the limits of relativism."

I use the title "Badrul Mustafa's Horse" for two different poems for a more lighthearted reason—not for the philosophical one above. In these two poems, I have used it only to show the difference in the relationships between horse and human. In the first, the horse as an ill-treated creature, and in the second, the horse as a creature bold enough to oppose its owner by breaking a promise or an engagement."

GAF: In "On the Day of the Execution," am I mistaken, but doesn't the shape-shifting Badrul Mustafa, now a general, seem to the reader rather uncharacteristically sympathetic, or perhaps, just pathetic?

HJP: Yes. This poem does seem rather stand-alone. Still, I wrote it without shifting from the spirit of this book. I wanted to describe a person of power (the General) in the final moments of his authority and power (the Day of Execution).

From the perspective of General Badrul Mustafa: I wanted to create a sort of irony of authority and power, especially when exercised by the hardline approach—military, Islamic fundamentalism, and the like. Like Soeharto, undeniably a killer, corruptor, and of course an authoritarian, who when his authority ended evoked humanitarianism to make himself look "humane" and thus to legitimize himself, as though the violence he and his ilk perpetrated while in power can be forgotten just like that. I am not teaching vengeance. I still believe that seeking pardon is necessary. But seeking pardon is an ethical question, while the wickedness of power that has tormented people cannot be resolved simply by saying "Sorry!", let alone if "Sorry!" comes at the end of a regime that is on the verge of collapse. In other words, I find it ironic when war criminals or "truth criminals" only become "aware of the importance of love" when their power collapses.

From the perspective of the Executioner: I use the image of General Badrul Mustafa to show the irony of authority and power, and I use the image of the executioner to show the next irony—that is, when an authority ends, it doesn't mean the one who assumes the power (the Executioner) is necessarily good. In my poetry, I show that wicked power is replaced by a newer wicked power (a general is replaced by an executioner). In retrospect, of course, this poem appears to show sympathy for the General Badrul Mustafa, but in the poem, I strongly wish to show that "the sweet nothings of love" can be a sort of gimmick to cover up greater things. Behind the General's sweet nothings of love, there is in fact a power struggle going on or a change of power from one military man to another one.

GAF: In "Just Like Badrul Mustafa," the poem seems to me to be a mystically ecstatic celebration of one's union with God. Sufistic, perhaps? But how, indeed, "Just like Badrul Mustafa"? He doesn't really appear in this poem.

HJP: An interesting view, and it could perhaps be like that. However, I wrote that poem to show how someone who previously had been strong, had felt himself as possessing authority and the truth, but then experienced moments of weakness, helplessness and self-doubt. I emphasize this by the end of the poem "Standing strong like a banyan in the market square / To be brought low by a passing breeze (*Teguh sudah bagai beringin tengah pasar, hendak rubuh oleh semisal angin sebentar*). Someone full of power may in time come to moments of weakness and helplessness. I imagine Badrul Mustafa—or maybe even hardliners—will be like that, too. No matter how strong they are now (like a mighty banyan tree), they will be overthrown in time. How can they be overthrown? The poem "Felling a Banyan Tree" attempts to answer that.

GAF: The "Rubaiyat of a Wanderer's Kopiah" is intensely interesting for a number of reasons, not least for the unusual element of history and foreign presence in it, along with some hyperbole about BMs prowess as a traveler to the Holy Land. But I am in the dark as to what this poem signifies. Perhaps, without giving too much away, you could provide some illumination on how a reader might approach this one. There's a lot in it, for sure.

HJP: The basic assumption I used when writing "The Rubaiyat of a Wanderer's Kopiah" was a condition in which society is taken in by fairytales, myths and legends, all spiced with religion (going on the hajj in a kopiah, not a ship, for example) and missing the facts before its collective eyes (living under colonialism). In today's context, "heavenly hopes and expectations" that Islamic fundamentalism provides make people forget other facts and realities no less important: social injustice, destruction of the forests, and so forth. Society at large is more afraid of losing their "religious fairytales" symbolized by the story of the kopiah, than the future of their lives, which is broken (damaged crops, devastated nature, and so forth).

Translated from the Indonesian by George A. Fowler

Biographical Information

The Author

Heru Joni Putra was born on October 13, 1990 in Payakumbuh, West Sumatra, Indonesia, the son of a local journalist and a farmer. He was raised in the Minangkabau culture, historically an arena of contention between various ideas about Islam, communism, and nationalism in Indonesia. He grew up in the midst of a never-ending tension between the Minangkabau language—which is filled with various literary devices, and dialect also dense in satire and sarcasm—and Bahasa Indonesia, the national language, which, according to Heru, was used feudally by the New Order regime (1966–1998) as a tool for social discipline.

In 2015, he completed his undergraduate studies in the Department of English Literature, the Faculty of Humanities, Universitas Andalas (Padang, West Sumatra), and in 2019, he completed post-graduate studies in Cultural Studies in the Faculty of Humanities, University of Indonesia in Jakarta. His first book, *Badrul Mustafa Badrul Mustafa Badrul Mustafa* (Bandung: Nuansa Cendekia, 2017) was described by the literary critic Nirwan Dewanto as a work of poetry that was outside the two main poetic traditions of Indonesia, that is, lyric poetry and pamphlet poetry. This book was awarded as the Best Book of Poetry by *Tempo* magazine in 2017, the Best Literary in the Wisran Hadi Award of 2019, and entered the shortlist of the 2017 Khatulistiwa Literary Award in two categories, Poetry and First Book.

The Translator

George A Fowler is a full-time freelance commercial and literary translator of Chinese, Indonesian, Malay, and Tagalog. His numerous published literary translations include *Sitti Nurbaya* by Marah Rusli (The Lontar Foundation, 2009), *Old Town* by Lin Zhe (Amazon Crossing, 2011), and *Islam, Humanity and the Indonesian Identity: Reflections on History (Debates on Islam and Society)* by Ahmad Syafii Maarif (Leiden University Press, 2018).

As well as having studied and worked for thirty years in the Asia-Pacific region, he also received a B.A. from the University of Toronto (1975) and an M.A. from the Jackson School of International Studies at the University of Washington (2002).

George and his wife Scholastica Auyong live in Woodinville, WA., USA.

Publication History

All of the Indonesian language originals of the poems in this collection were first published in *Badrul Mustafa Badrul Mustafa Badrul Mustafa* (Bandung: Nuansa Cendekia, 2017). Translations with an asterisk after the title were first published in *The Mystical Path of Badrul Mustafa* (Jakarta: The Lontar Foundation, 2019). Many of these were slightly revised for this edition.

English Title	Original Title
The Beard of Haji Agus Salim *	Jenggot Haji Agus Salim
Where There Is No Forest, a City Will Do	Tak Ada Rimba, Kota pun Jadi
Ballad of the Gold-Embroidered Rag	Ballada Kain Buruk Bersulam Emas
Dancing on a Weathered Footbridge *	Berjoged di Atas Titian Lapuk
Just Call This Poem "Meditation" *	Beri Saja Judul Puisi Ini Meditasi
Ballad of the Tree Stump *	Balada Tunggul Kayu
It's Out, the Torch In Hand *	Sudah Padam Suluh di Tangan
Killing the Court Poet	Membunuh Pujangga Istana
Ballad of the Torn Sandal *	Balada Sandal Putus
Badrul Mustafa's Horse, 1 *	Kuda Badrul Mustafa
Badrul Mustafa's Horse, 2 *	Kuda Badrul Mustafa
Badrul Mustafa Falls In Love Again *	Badrul Mustafa Jatuh Cinta Lagi
Only the Scent Remains	Rendang Tinggal Dedak
Learning to Recite to a Cow Pen *	Belajar Mengaji ke Kandang Sapi
Ballad of the Lunatic Who Mounted the Pulpit	Balada Orang Gila Naik Mimbar
Riding a Shipwreck	Bersampan Dengan Pecahan Kapal
Ballad of the Man Who Was an Admirer of Jibril *	Balada Lelaki Pengagum Jibril
Song of the Sword Grinder	Lagu Pengasah Pedang
Song of the Farmer without a Field	Lagu Petani Tak Bersawah
A Storyteller without Applause *	Juru Cerita Tanpa Tepuk Tangan

English Title	Original Title
Ballad of the Paper Lion	Balada Singa Ompong
Ballad of the Deer With the Broken Leg	Balada Rusa Patah Kaki
Ballad of the Monkey Who Got a Toy, 1	Balada Beruk Mendapat Permainan
Ballad of the Monkey Who Got a Toy, 2 *	Balada Beruk Mendapat Permainan
At the Tomb of a Padri	Di Makam Seorang Padri
On the Day of the Execution	Di Hari Eksekusi Itu
An Elephant Across the Sea and an Ant Across the Sea *	Gajah di Seberang Lautan dan Semut di Seberang Lautan
Spellbound by a Tiger	Pukau Harimau
Frog On a Coconut Shell *	Katak di Atas Tempurung
A Body That Doesn't Know Itself *	Badan yang Tak Tahu Diri
Just Like Badrul Mustafa	Semisal Badrul Mustafa
A Thorn In the Flesh	Duri Dalam Daging
At a Café	Pada Sebuah Cafe
The Rubaiyat of a Wanderer's Kopiah *	Rubaiyat Anak Dagang
Return of the Adept	Jalan Pulang Orang Suluk
Salt and Ants	Ada Garam Ada Semut
Prawn Before a Stone	Udang di Depan Batu
Waiting for the Fighters to Enter the Arena *	Menunggu Pendekar Masuk Gelang-gang
Padri Cheerleader *	Tukang Sorak Kaum Padri
Badrul Mustafa Will Never Die	Badrul Mustafa Will Never Die
Felling a Banyan Tree	Menumbangkan Pohon Beringin
At a Café	Pada Sebuah Cafe
The Rubaiyat of a Wanderer's Kopiah *	Rubaiyat Anak Dagang
Return of the Adept	Jalan Pulang Orang Suluk
Salt and Ants	Ada Garam Ada Semut
Prawn Before a Stone	Udang di Depan Batu
Waiting for the Fighters to Enter the Arena *	Menunggu Pendekar Masuk Gelang-gang
Padri Cheerleader *	Tukang Sorak Kaum Padri
Badrul Mustafa Will Never Die	Badrul Mustafa Will Never Die
Felling a Banyan Tree	Menumbangkan Pohon Beringin

www.ingramcontent.com/pod-product-compliance
Lightning Source LLC
Chambersburg PA
CBHW031330230926
51848CB00001B/170
9786237150152